BY JAKE MADDOX

TEXT BY
SCOTT WELVAERT

ILLUSTRATIONS BY
SEAN TIFFANY

STONE ARCH BOOKS
a capstone imprint

Jake Maddox books are published by Stone Arch Books
A Capstone Imprint
1710 Roe Crest Drive
North Mankato, Minnesota 56003
www.capstonepub.com

Library of Congress Cataloging-in-Publication Data
Maddox, Jake.
Behind the plate / by Jake Maddox; text by Chris Kreie; illustrated by Sean
Tiffany.
p. cm. — (Jake Maddox sports story)
ISBN 978-1-4342-4010-1 (library binding) — ISBN 978-1-4342-4205-1 (pbk.)
1. Baseball stories. 2. Stress (Psychology)—Juvenile fiction. 3. Children of divorced
parents—Juvenile fiction. 4. Fathers and sons—Juvenile fiction. [1. Baseball—
Fiction. 2. Stress (Psychology)—Fiction. 3. Divorce—Fiction. 4. Fathers and sons—
Fiction.] I. Kreie, Chris. II. Tiffany, Sean, ill. III. Title.
PZ7.M25643Beh 2012
813.6—dc23   2011053322

Graphic Designer: Russell Griesmer
Production Specialist: Danielle Ceminsky

Photo Credits: Shutterstock/Ozerov Alexander 41899459 (Cover), Shutterstock
43565725 (p. 66, 72), Shutterstock/Nicemonkey 71713762 (p. 3)

Printed in China.
032012
006677RRDF12

TABLE OF CONTENTS

CHAPTER 1
A PROBLEM THROWING

Danny crouched behind home plate. His left arm was extended in front of him. His right hand was tucked behind his glove. His catcher's mitt was open and ready for the ball.

His teammate Jack stood on the pitcher's mound. Jack went into his windup. Danny sat steady and still, but his heart raced. He couldn't wait for what was about to happen.

The ball flew through the air and popped into Danny's glove. He sprang out of his crouch like a lion after its prey. In one fluid motion, he grabbed the ball, reached his hand behind his head, and gunned a throw to second base.

His mask twisted sideways on his face. Danny ripped the mask away so he could watch the flight of the ball.

His teammate Mike ran over from his position between first and second base to make the catch. Danny watched as the ball landed in Mike's glove. It was close to the ground and just a foot away from the base.

"Great throw!" shouted Mike.

"Great catch!" yelled Danny. He pulled his mask back on and returned to his position behind the plate.

It was the first practice of the season. Danny felt good. He loved this drill. He could hardly wait to throw real base runners out in a game.

"Time for pitchers' practice," called Coach Byrd.

"Just one more?" asked Danny. He stood up and pleaded with his coach. "I think I can get the ball even closer to the bag."

"Okay, one more," said Coach Byrd, smiling. "But our pitchers need a workout, too."

"Thanks, Coach," Danny said, returning to his crouch.

Jack lobbed another ball from the pitcher's mound. Danny caught it and repeated his routine.

He fired another throw to second base. This time the ball landed only inches off the plate. The infielder let out a whoop as he caught the ball and put the tag on an invisible runner.

"Great job, Danny," said Coach Byrd.

"Another perfect play," said Alex, walking toward the mound. "Now, are you ready for some perfect pitches?"

"Bring 'em on!" said Danny.

Danny and Alex were best friends, and they had been teammates for three years. Alex was the star pitcher, and Danny was the Dodgers' starting catcher.

They were an amazing combination. The year before, their team had advanced far into the playoffs, just missing the championship round.

Alex and Danny were determined to help the Dodgers go all the way this season.

Alex stood on the mound, and Danny waited for his throw. "Let's see what you've got!" Danny yelled.

Alex unleashed the pitch. The ball shot from his hand like a rubber band. Danny remained in his squat as the ball smacked hard into his glove.

"Nice!" Danny said. "I think you've picked up some speed over the winter."

Danny stood up and started to toss the ball back to Alex. Suddenly his arm went limp. Something didn't feel right.

He let go of the ball, but the throw felt funny. The ball bounced twice in the dirt before rolling to Alex's feet.

"What was that?" asked Alex.

Danny shook his head. He stretched out his throwing arm. "I guess I'm just tired from practice," he said.

Alex laughed, and then prepared for his next throw. He fired another pitch, and again Danny stood and tossed the ball back to Alex. This time his throw was even worse. The ball rolled into the grass in front of the mound.

"What the heck?" Danny said to himself.

"Come on," said Alex. "You can fire a bullet to second, but you can't make a simple toss to me? Quit goofing around."

"I'm not," said Danny.

Alex let another pitch fly, and another. Both times, Danny's throws back to him were off target.

"Are you okay?" asked Coach Byrd.

"I'm fine," said Danny. "Pitch me another one, Alex."

Alex reared back and threw one more fastball. This time Danny stood up slowly. He concentrated on the throw. He did not want to miss Alex again.

Danny cocked his arm behind his body, reached forward, and let go of the ball. It sailed high into the air, up and over Alex's outstretched glove. Danny just stared in disbelief.

"Take a break," said Coach Byrd.

"But I can do it," said Danny. "I know I can."

"I know you can, too," said Coach Byrd. "Just take a few laps around the field. Then come back and we'll try again."

"But . . ." said Danny.

"But nothing," said Coach Byrd. "Start running. That's an order."

Danny walked into the dugout and removed his catching gear. As he jogged into the outfield, he thought about what had happened.

He had no idea what was wrong. The difficult throws were easy to make, but suddenly the easy throws had become nearly impossible.

CHAPTER 2
TO RIGHT FIELD

A week later, Danny and Alex stood together on the pitcher's mound. The Dodgers were warming up for the season's first game. They were getting ready to play the White Sox.

Danny had struggled in every practice leading up to the game. Most of his throws to the mound had been fine. But every now and then, he would throw a ball over the pitcher's head or into the dirt at the pitcher's feet. He'd made mistakes he shouldn't have made.

"What if I can't throw back to you?" Danny asked Alex as they warmed up. "What if I screw up?"

"You won't," said Alex. "When it's game time, you're always in the zone."

"I hope you're right," said Danny.

"Play ball!" shouted the umpire.

Danny turned and jogged toward home. "I can do this," he said to himself. "I've made these throws all my life. There's nothing to it."

He placed his right arm behind his back and extended his glove hand in front of his body. He waited for Alex to make the delivery.

The ball came in hard. The White Sox batter swung quickly and pounded a hard shot over the third baseman.

As the Dodgers' left fielder ran to collect the ball, the hitter made it to second base with ease. It was a leadoff double.

Danny immediately began to worry about the runner on second. He thought about his throwing problems and let out a deep breath.

"Here we go," he said.

Alex paused on the mound and then went into his windup. He gunned the ball toward home. Danny waited. The batter watched the pitch sail outside for a ball.

Danny easily caught the ball. *It's just an easy throw to the pitcher*, he thought. *There's nothing to it.*

He reached back, but something wasn't right. His arm felt like a wet noodle. He released the ball.

Right away, he could tell that his throw was going to be bad. And he was right. Alex couldn't catch it. The ball glanced off his glove and dribbled into short right field. The runner on second base saw his chance. He ran to third.

From there, things only got worse. On the next pitch, Danny was so focused on making a good throw to Alex that he didn't even catch the ball. It slipped under his glove and rolled to the backstop.

The runner from third came across home plate to score. It was 1 to 0, only one White Sox player had batted, and Danny had already committed two errors. The game wasn't looking good.

Danny made two more throwing errors and the White Sox scored three more times before the Dodgers finally earned three outs.

As the Dodgers walked slowly into the dugout, Coach Byrd followed Danny. "I'm moving you to right field," Coach Byrd said.

"Right field?" asked Danny. "But I'm a catcher."

"Not today," said Coach Byrd. "I'm sorry, but we can't risk any more errors."

"I'll do better," said Danny.

"Yes, you will," said Coach Byrd. "You'll do better next game. For now, I need you in right."

Danny sat down on the bench next to Alex. "I'm jinxed," he said.

"Don't worry," said Alex, laughing. "You're too good to be playing so bad."

"Thanks a lot," Danny said, leaning his head against the dugout wall.

CHAPTER 3
THE YIPS

The next morning, Danny pedaled his bike across town. The team had the day off. He planned to spend it with his dad.

Even though Danny was happy to get a break from the baseball field, a different sort of problem lay ahead of him. Danny's mom and dad had gotten divorced a few months earlier. And lately nothing had been easy between Danny and his dad. Every minute they spent together was awkward.

Danny pulled up to the two-story apartment building and locked his bike to the fence. The brick building was old. The bushes near the walls were overgrown and needed to be trimmed.

He entered the building and met his dad outside his apartment door. The two of them hugged. "It's good to see you, kiddo," said his dad. "Come on in."

The apartment was small, and it smelled a little like old socks. But Danny wanted to be upbeat. "Nice place," he said.

"Thanks," said Dad. "I was hoping you would like it. There's a pool, too. And even a basketball court. We can shoot some hoops later."

"Cool," said Danny. He set his bag on the floor and sat down on the sofa. "The furniture's nice," he said.

Dad laughed. "I like it," he said. "But I'm not sure all the pieces match. Your mom was always the one with the style in our house." He paused. "Speaking of your mom, how is she?"

"She's good," said Danny.

Dad sat down in a chair across from him. "And how are you?" he asked. He leaned forward. "Are you still seeing that counselor at school?"

"I'm fine," said Danny. He squirmed in his chair. There were several seconds of silence. Finally, Danny looked at his dad and gave him a weak smile. "Can we talk about something else?" Danny asked.

"I'm sorry," said Dad. He got up from his chair. "You just got here. I shouldn't be asking you so many questions."

His dad went into the kitchen and came back with two cans of soda. "What should we talk about?" Dad asked.

Danny opened his can and took a long drink. "I have a baseball problem. Maybe you can help me with it," he said.

"Sure," said his dad. "What is it?"

"I'm having trouble throwing to the mound," said Danny.

"You mean throwing back to your pitcher?" asked Dad.

"Yeah," said Danny. "My throws are either super short or they fly off in the wrong direction. It's driving me crazy."

"That's the yips," said his dad, nodding.

"The what?" Danny asked. "Are you being serious?"

"Totally serious. The yips are when a ball player suddenly has difficulty making routine plays," Dad said. "It happens in baseball and in golf and in all sorts of sports."

Danny frowned. "I've never heard of the yips," he said.

"It's pretty common," Dad said. "I bet there's information on the Internet that could help you. Why don't you do some research? I'll make us some lunch." Dad went back into the kitchen. Then he called out, "Does grilled cheese sound okay?"

"Sure," said Danny.

Danny looked around at the tiny apartment. So much in his life had changed. He wanted his old life back. He wanted his old dad back. And he didn't want to have the yips.

CHAPTER 4
TIPS TO BEAT THE YIPS

Later that evening, Danny and Alex were back at the ballpark. Danny was behind home plate. Alex was on the mound. He was holding a printout of an article Danny had found online.

"It's called 'the yips,' huh?" said Alex. "That's a weird name. It sounds like a disease."

"I know," said Danny. "But a whole bunch of guys have had them."

Danny started listing players. "Chuck Knoblauch for the Yankees, Steve Sax for the L.A. Dodgers, and Rick Ankiel for the Cardinals," he said. "The article says that some players get the yips because of an injury, a traumatic event, or because of personal stress."

"Then there's just one question," said Alex. "Can you beat the yips?"

"I'm going to try my hardest," said Danny. "Let's go."

"Okay," said Alex. He looked at the article. "It says here you need to visualize yourself throwing the ball back to the mound before you throw it. Picture yourself making the perfect throw to your pitcher."

"Right," said Danny. "Put the paper down. Let's try it."

Alex grabbed a ball and got ready to throw it. "Picture yourself throwing now!" he yelled.

Danny took a deep breath and pictured himself making an easy toss back to Alex. He imagined his arm going back and then gently moving forward as he snapped his wrist and released the ball. It seemed so easy.

"Okay!" he shouted to Alex.

Alex threw him a pitch. Danny caught it and stood up for the throw. He reached back and tried to recreate the picture he had just seen in his mind. Finally, he let go of the ball. It missed Alex's glove by six feet and rolled toward the infield.

"Shoot," Danny muttered.

"It's just one throw," said Alex, running after the ball. "Let's try it again."

"It didn't work," Danny said. "Let's try something else."

Alex grabbed the article. "Another trick is to clear your mind," he said. "Try not to think about the throw."

"First it says to think about the throw," said Danny. "Then it says to not think about it. Maybe this article is a waste of time."

"I thought you said you wanted to beat the yips," said Alex.

"I do," said Danny. "Okay. I'll clear my mind. But how?"

"You're supposed to think of something completely different from baseball," said Alex. "Like a sunny beach or your favorite food or a cute girl." He looked at Danny. "You should think about Emily Akers from biology."

"I'll think about a hot fudge sundae," said Danny.

"Whatever," said Alex with a shrug. He tossed Danny the ball.

"Rich chocolate," Danny whispered to himself. "Smooth ice cream. Peanuts." He caught the ball. "And thick whipped cream."

He moved the ball to his right hand and sent it back to Alex. The ball sailed three feet over Alex's head.

"I *told* you to think about Emily," said Alex, laughing.

Danny shook his head. "What's next?" he asked. "I have to figure this out."

"You need to have patience," said Alex. "Give these cures some time."

"I don't have time. Our next game is tomorrow," said Danny. "I need to get better. Now."

Alex read more from the article. "Okay, listen to this one," he said. "I think you're going to like it. It doesn't involve thinking or not thinking."

"Sounds good so far," said Danny.

"It says that before you throw the ball, you should smack it into your glove a couple of times," Alex said.

"Why?" asked Danny.

"It's supposed to make you focus on the smacking instead of the throwing," said Alex.

"Okay, I'll try it," said Danny. "I like that one."

Alex set himself on the mound as Danny went into his crouch. Alex leaned back and lobbed the ball to home.

Danny caught it, and then got to his feet. "Here goes," he whispered.

SMACK! SMACK! He pounded the ball into his glove, and then tossed it back to Alex. The throw was perfect.

"That's what I'm talking about!" shouted Alex.

"Yes!" said Danny. "It worked! Let's try it again."

Alex pitched several more strikes to Danny. Each time, Danny smacked the ball into his glove twice. Then he made a perfect throw back to the mound.

"You're back!" shouted Alex.

"Finally!" Danny said. He smiled. He felt more relaxed than he had all season.

"Now feel my heater," said Alex as he went into his windup.

"Bring it on!" yelled Danny.

Alex let go of the ball. It flew toward home plate and popped loudly into Danny's glove. "Nice!" shouted Danny.

He stood up. He pounded the ball into his glove. Then he threw it back to Alex. To Danny's horror, the ball sailed wildly into the outfield. He brought both hands to his head. "Not again!" he moaned.

Alex shook his head. "It looks like we need to find another cure," he said. "Your yips are pretty bad."

CHAPTER 5
THE CAUSE

Danny sat on the pitcher's mound. "What am I going to do?" he asked. "My baseball career is dead."

"No, it's not," said Alex. "I'm sure you'll get rid of your yips eventually."

The two of them sat for a while in the middle of the baseball field. Danny grabbed pebbles from the dirt around the mound and tried to make them land on home plate.

"I wonder what made this happen, anyway," Danny said. "It's so weird." He threw a rock, and it landed perfectly on the plate.

Both boys laughed. "You can't hit my glove to save your life," said Alex. "But you can put a tiny rock on a seventeen-inch base from fifty feet away."

"Yeah," said Danny. He threw some more stones.

"Wait a minute," said Alex. "What did you just say?"

"I agreed with you," said Danny. "It's funny that I can throw a rock onto home plate, but I can't land a baseball in your glove."

"No," said Alex. "Before that."

"Um," said Danny, "I was wondering what caused the yips."

"That's it!" Alex said. He reached over and grabbed the printout of the article.

"What's it?" asked Danny.

Alex read from the article. "'The yips can be caused by an injury, a traumatic event, or personal stress,'" he read. "'A player may experience something in his life that has nothing to do with the sport, but it causes his mind and body to stop performing on the field.'"

"What about it?" asked Danny.

"Don't you get it?" said Alex. "It says a traumatic event or stress could be the reason."

"Yeah . . . so?" said Danny.

Alex repeated the words slowly, with expression. "A traumatic event." He stared at Danny.

Suddenly Danny understood. His eyes went wide. "My parents' divorce," he said.

"That's what probably caused your yips," said Alex.

Danny looked at the ground. He didn't like to think about the divorce. In fact, for the past few months he had tried really hard to forget all about it.

"Are you still mad at your dad for leaving?" asked Alex. He dug another rock out of the ground. "I know I would be."

Danny looked up. He didn't say anything.

"If you're mad, you should probably tell him," said Alex.

Danny just shook his head. "What am I supposed to say?" he asked. "'You messed everything up.' No way."

Alex paused. "But don't you think —"

Danny interrupted him. "That the divorce is causing my throwing problems?" He let out a deep breath. "Yeah, maybe," he said. "It makes sense. My dad and I never talk about the divorce. Whenever we try to, the conversation just dies."

"You guys used to talk about everything," said Alex.

Danny stood up and began to walk away.

"Where are you going?" asked Alex.

Danny hopped onto his bike. "I'm going to my dad's office," he said.

"Now?" Alex asked.

"If we're going to win tomorrow, I need to take care of this today," said Danny.

CHAPTER 6
GAME ON

Alex was already at the baseball field when Danny arrived the next morning. "Did you talk to your dad?" Alex asked. "How did it go?"

Danny got off his bike and slung his bat bag onto the ground. He pulled a glove and ball from his bag. He started walking toward the backstop. "It went well," he said, smiling.

"Yeah?" said Alex.

"Really well," said Danny. His smile got even bigger.

"That's great," said Alex. "How did your dad handle it when you told him how you felt?"

"It was tough," said Danny. "There was a lot of blubbering and hugging and all that. But it was good. My dad and I got a lot of things figured out. He's coming to the game later."

"Awesome," said Alex, running past Danny onto the field. "So let's go play some ball."

"It's about time!" shouted Danny.

* * *

By the top of the third inning, they led the Rays 2 to 0. Alex was pitching a great game. He struck out the first eight batters.

Danny had driven in two runs with a double in the bottom of the first. And to make things even better, he had not thrown one bad ball all game.

It probably helped that his dad had been there to cheer him on. Danny knew things would never be the same as they were before the divorce, but he was glad that he and his dad were starting to talk again. It was a big first step.

With two outs in the inning, Danny sat behind the plate and waited for Alex to go into his windup. The Rays batter stood tall in the batter's box.

Alex kicked and threw. The batter shifted his weight from his back leg to his front leg and gracefully swung the bat. Danny closed his glove, but the ball never got there. The batter hit a solid line drive into the outfield.

The Rays players hooted and hollered as the Dodgers' left fielder threw the ball to second base. The Rays batter jogged into first base with a single.

Danny stood behind the plate as the ball was thrown back to Alex. Danny pulled his mask back from his face. He couldn't help staring at the runner on first. It was the first time a Rays player had gotten a hit all game.

Danny took a deep breath. Throwing with the bases empty was easy. The true test was whether he could keep making good throws with a runner on base.

He turned to Alex, who was holding his throwing hand palm down. Danny knew that Alex was telling him to relax. Danny nodded and stepped back behind home plate.

Make a good throw, Danny thought.
*Catch the ball and throw it to Alex. There's
nothing to it.*

Alex went into his windup. Danny
caught the next pitch after the batter
watched it go by. Strike one. Danny stood
up and made a casual throw. It landed
perfectly in Alex's glove. "Yes," he said to
himself, smiling.

It wasn't until Alex caught the ball that
Danny noticed the Rays player sliding
feet-first into second base. The runner had
stolen second, and Danny had completely
missed it.

He felt terrible. He had been so focused
on getting the ball back to Alex that he
had completely ignored the runner.

"Let's pay attention out there!" Coach
Byrd, yelled from the dugout.

"It's okay," Alex shouted from the mound. "No problem."

Danny nodded and got back into position. He couldn't wait for the inning to be over. He didn't want to make an error and allow the Rays to get a run.

Alex kicked and threw. This time Danny watched the whole field. He saw the runner on second take off to try and steal third.

Danny caught the pitch. Then he stood and gunned the ball to third base. The runner slid head-first into the bag. The ball arrived just a split-second too late.

"Safe!" yelled the umpire.

"Shoot," muttered Danny.

"Catcher!" Alex shouted from the mound. He waved for Danny to join him.

"Time," said Danny. He raised both hands into the air.

"Time!" shouted the home plate umpire.

Danny jogged to the mound.

"Shake it off," Alex said. "That wasn't your fault. That guy is quick."

"I know," said Danny.

"You're doing fine," said Alex. "You haven't made one bad throw yet." He smacked Danny in the chest with his glove. "You can do this," he added.

"You're right," Danny said. "I can."

"Great," said Alex. "Let's go!"

Danny turned and trotted back to the plate. As the Rays batter took some practice swings, Danny tried to build back his confidence.

"Let's do this thing," he whispered.
"There's nothing to it."

Alex leaned forward and stared toward home. Danny's heart was thumping hard in his chest. Alex stood up straight, then began his windup. Danny waited with his glove extended.

The ball came flying from Alex's hand. The batter cocked his bat and swung. *CRACK!*

The ball sailed toward left field. The batter had hit the ball hard, but it had popped up high into the air. The left fielder would be able to make a play.

Danny watched as the ball fell from the sky. The runner at third took a few steps back and put his toe on the bag. He was tagging up.

Danny knew that once the ball was caught, the runner would be able to try to run home.

The ball landed in the outfielder's glove. And sure enough, the runner took off. He sprinted directly toward Danny.

Danny set himself in front of home plate as his teammate released a throw from left. It was a good throw. Danny tried to keep his eye on the ball and not get distracted by the runner. He knew if he dropped the ball, it wouldn't matter how good the throw was.

The play was going to be close. Danny could tell. The runner was almost to home as the ball landed in Danny's glove.

In one quick move, he caught the ball and swept his glove toward the plate, tagging the Rays player on the foot.

"Out!" shouted the umpire.

The Dodgers cheered and pumped their fists. Danny stood up, slammed the ball to the ground and sprinted to the dugout.

His dad shouted to him from the bleachers. "Great job, Danny!" he yelled.

Danny looked up and smiled. Alex ran up to him with a high-five. "Game on," said Alex.

"Game on," said Danny.

CHAPTER 7
UP TO BAT

Things tightened up in the next few innings. Alex continued to pitch well, but the Rays found a way to put two runs on the board. When the Dodgers prepared to bat at the bottom of the sixth inning, the game was tied 2 to 2.

Danny felt great. He had been making good throws back to the mound. The yips finally seemed to be over.

Alex stepped up to the plate to bat. Danny stood in the on-deck circle, waiting for his turn to hit. "Come on, Alex!" he shouted. He felt comfortable and happy. It was like the yips had never happened.

On the first pitch, Alex hit a line drive into the gap between center field and right field. He ran hard past first base. He made it to second with a leadoff double.

"That's the way to do it!" yelled Danny. His teammates cheered behind him as he stepped up to the plate. "Time to drive him home," he told himself.

Danny waited patiently in the batter's box and took a few practice swings. Alex took a healthy lead off second base.

The pitcher finally went into his windup. Danny waited as the ball soared toward him. He was ready.

At the perfect moment, he cocked his bat and drove his back foot into the ground. All his energy went forward as he swung the bat. The ball slammed off his bat and over the head of the pitcher. The shortstop and the second baseman ran toward the ball, but it shot between them and into center field.

Danny ran to first just as the center fielder got the ball. Alex raced around third and flew toward home. The center fielder threw the ball to the catcher just as Alex slid into home. In a cloud of dirt and dust, the umpire made the call. "Safe!" he yelled.

The Dodgers players went crazy. Danny pumped his fist at first base as Alex pointed out to him. Danny pointed back and grinned. He had driven in an important run. The Dodgers were ahead, 3 to 2.

The inning ended quickly after that. The next two Dodgers batters went down swinging, and the last batter of the inning made the final out on a lazy fly ball to left. Danny and Alex had done their jobs. If the Dodgers kept the Rays from scoring their next time up to bat, the game would be over. The Dodgers would have their win.

CHAPTER 8
THE BIG FINISH

In the seventh and final inning, Danny suited up in his catching gear as Alex returned to the mound. He clipped on his chest protector, placed his helmet on his head, and pulled his mask down over his face.

"Play ball!" shouted the umpire.

The first Rays batter struck out. The second batter popped out on a fly ball. Danny caught the ball for out number two. The game was almost over.

"One more out!" shouted Danny as he made an effortless throw to the mound. His yips were far away now. He didn't have to worry about them anymore.

Danny positioned himself behind the plate and watched as the next Rays batter stepped into the box. He was confident this would be the last batter of the game.

But he was wrong. The batter hit a line drive over the mound, and the next batter squeaked a hit between second and third base.

Just like that, the Rays had runners on first and third. With another hit, the player at third could score and the game would be tied.

Danny pushed his mask off his face and took a couple of steps in front of the plate.

"You can do this!" he shouted to Alex. "Don't worry about the runners. Just get this next guy."

Alex nodded, and Danny returned to his position. As he crouched, Danny glanced toward the runner at first base. Then he took a quick look at the runner on third.

"Play your game," he whispered to himself. "Your arm is as strong as ever."

Alex stood on the mound for several seconds.

Danny slowly tucked his throwing hand behind his glove and extended his left arm in front of him.

Alex peered into the box. He went into his slow windup.

Danny waited.

The world went quiet. Danny kept his glove slightly open, ready for the pitch. He held his breath as Alex kicked and threw.

Then he saw it.

The runner on first had broken into a sprint. He was trying to steal second.

Danny had only an instant to think as Alex's pitch flew toward him. A bad throw to second meant the runner at third would score and the game would be tied. But a good throw meant an out. And an out meant the game would be over. Danny knew what he had to do.

The batter swung at the ball and missed.

Danny caught the ball. He jumped out of his crouch and gunned a throw toward second.

The shortstop ran over to make the play. The Rays runner charged hard toward second base.

The runner slid into second base feet-first as the shortstop caught the ball and tagged him. Danny knew it was going to be close.

The umpire leaned in toward second base. His right fist shot into the air. "Out!" he yelled.

The Dodgers shortstop held the ball high over his head and jumped into the air in victory. Danny raced out to the mound. The rest of his teammates joined him in a mob around Alex.

"We beat the Rays!" shouted Alex. "We actually did it!"

"Thanks to your awesome pitching!" said Danny.

"And your awesome throwing," said Alex. "I think you finally beat the yips."

"The yips?" said Danny. He smiled. "What are those?" He and Alex laughed. "But now we have a new challenge," Danny said.

"What's that?" asked Alex.

"Winning the city championship!" yelled Danny.

"I like the sound of that!" Alex replied. Together, they walked off the field in victory.

ABOUT THE AUTHOR

Chris Kreie lives in Minnesota with his wife and two children. He is an avid fan of all sports, but baseball is one of his favorites. His greatest baseball memory is attending the World Series with his dad in 1991 and seeing the Minnesota Twins win Game 7. Chris is also the author of *Gridiron Bully*, *Hockey Meltdown*, and *Pitcher Pressure* from the Jake Maddox series.

ABOUT THE ILLUSTRATOR

When Sean Tiffany was growing up, he lived on a small island off the coast of Maine. Every day, from sixth grade until he graduated from high school, he had to take a boat to get to school. When Sean isn't working on his art, he works on a multimedia project called "OilCan Drive," which combines music and art. He has a pet cactus named Jim.

GLOSSARY

concentrated (KON-suhn-tray-ted)—focused your thoughts and attention on something

errors (ER-urz)—misplays made by a fielder in baseball

fly ball (FLYE BAWLL)—a ball hit high in the air

leadoff double (LEED-awf DUH-buhl)—a hit where the first batter in the lineup safely makes it to second base

line drive (LINE DRIVE)—a baseball hit in a nearly straight line usually not far above the ground

routine (roo-TEEN)—a regular way or pattern of doing things

traumatic (traw-MAT-ik)—shocking and very upsetting

DISCUSSION QUESTIONS

1. Did Coach Byrd do enough to help Danny with his yips?

2. Have you ever experienced the yips or something similar? Do you know someone who has? What happened?

3. Do you think that Danny should have talked to his dad about the divorce earlier? Why or why not?

WRITING PROMPTS

1. Pretend you are Danny and you have just finished the game against the White Sox. Coach Byrd moved you to right field instead of catcher. Write a journal entry explaining how you feel.

2. Choose one of the cures for the yips that are discussed in Chapter 4. Write a persuasive paragraph to convince others that this is the best cure.

3. Danny had a hard time telling his dad what was bothering him. It may have been helpful for Danny to write a letter instead. Pretend you are Danny and write a letter to your dad.

Even major league baseball players can get the yips. When it happens, players often have to change their way of doing things. Sometimes it can even end their professional careers.

Pitcher Steve Blass helped lead the Pittsburgh Pirates to a World Series win in 1971. He pitched two complete games that series, and he allowed just two runs during those eighteen innings.

However, he suddenly lost control on the mound during the next season. He walked 84 players that year and struck out 27. He never really recovered and finally retired in 1975.

In 1983, Los Angeles Dodger second baseman Steve Sax had trouble with his throws to first base. He committed thirty errors that season, and the yips became known as "Steve Sax Syndrome."

Sax was able to work his way back, though. In 1989, he even led the American League in fielding percentage and double plays.

Chuck Knoblauch was one of the league's top second basemen before he developed the yips. As a New York Yankee in 1999, he began having problems throwing to first base. Sometimes the ball would even sail into the stands by mistake. Eventually, Knoblauch was moved to left field. He never returned to second base.

Rick Ankiel pitched for the St. Louis Cardinals for two years. Then, in 2001, he could no longer pitch strikes consistently. The team moved him back to the minor leagues, where he tried to get his pitching form back.

Finally, he made the move to the outfield. He returned to the Cardinals in 2007, batting second and playing right field.